Little Passports®
A GLOBAL ADVENTURE

The Mummy
Mix-Up

Written by AnnMarie Anderson

Illustrated by Carrie English

D1496056

4

Sam & Sofia's Scooter Stories

First paperback edition printed in 2020 by Little Passports, Inc.
Copyright © 2020 Little Passports
All rights reserved
Manufactured in China
10 9 8 7 6 5 4 3 2

Little Passports, Inc.
27 Maiden Lane, Suite 400, San Francisco, CA 94108
www.littlepassports.com
ISBN: 978-1-953148-03-2

Contents

1

Show-and-Tell

Sam flipped off the light switch, plunging Compass Community Center's theater into darkness. Sam's aunt Charlie stood on a small stage next to a white movie screen, illuminated by a beam of light.

"Welcome to today's show-and-tell about

1

ancient Egypt's greatest scientific mysteries," Aunt Charlie began.

Sam's best friend Sofia gave Aunt Charlie a thumbs-up from the back of the theater, where she operated the spotlight. She and Sam had volunteered to be the audiovisual team for Aunt Charlie's talk later that evening. They'd decided to come early to practice with the equipment.

"Let's begin with some footage from a research cruise I took on the Nile River many years ago," Aunt Charlie continued.

That was Sam's cue to turn on the film projector. Egypt's iconic pyramids appeared on

the screen, a few camels crossing the sandy desert in front of them. The hazy light of the flickering projector and the subdued colors of the film made Sam feel like he was standing right in front of the pyramids in the hot desert.

"Doesn't the footage look cool?" Sam whispered to Sofia. "Aunt Charlie shot this using an old movie camera called a Super 8."

Sofia nodded. "It makes the pyramids look extra special," she said.

"From Giza, our boat traveled south on the Nile River toward the city of Luxor," Aunt Charlie went on. The image on the screen changed. A wide dark-colored river replaced the pyramids. Water lapped against the shore, which was lined with green palm trees and lush plants.

"Does anyone know in which direction the Nile River flows?" Aunt Charlie asked.

Sofia's hand shot up.

"Yes?" Aunt Charlie said, raising her eyebrow at Sofia.

"It flows north," Sofia said.

"That's right!" Aunt Charlie exclaimed. "The Nile flows from the hilly lakes in the southern part of Africa's Rift Valley to the Mediterranean Sea in the north."

"Is that why the ancient Egyptians called the southern part of the country Upper Egypt and the northern part Lower Egypt?" Sam asked.

"It is!" Aunt Charlie replied. "I didn't know you'd been studying ancient Egypt, Sam."

Sam pulled a comic book from his messenger bag.

"I got this at the library," he explained.

Sofia read the cover aloud. "*Courageous Crosby's Hunt for the Lost Pyramid*."

Sam grinned. "It's about an adventurer who's searching for a legendary pyramid full of

ancient treasures. Her name is Cecilia Crosby, and she follows clues all over Egypt."

"Egypt is a fascinating place to explore." Aunt Charlie smiled at Sam. "You'll like this part of the presentation."

The image on the film changed again. The river was replaced with large paintings depicting ancient Egyptian life.

"And now we head to King Tut's tomb in Luxor," Aunt Charlie continued. "These paintings were found on the walls inside the tomb. See the brown spots? That's mold. Other tombs nearby are mold-free. Some scientists think, because King Tut died unexpectedly, the tomb was prepared quickly and sealed before the paint was dry."

"Wow," Sam murmured. "Scientists are like detectives!"

Aunt Charlie smiled. "Very true," she said. "Now, in a second you'll see my favorite part of the trip. The crocodile mummy is coming up, followed by my visit to the Temple of Kom Ombo near Aswan. It's the site of an ancient Egyptian calendar in hieroglyphics. Here it comes!"

The image on the screen cut from the smooth, dark river to an enormous ancient temple bathed in the pink light of the setting sun. Sam stared in awe, but a second later, the film darkened. He could no longer make out the temple, or anything else, for that matter. The picture was dark and shadowy.

"Oh no!" Aunt Charlie groaned. "Something must've happened to the film!"

2

A Super Idea

Sam flicked on the lights and looked at the projector.

"What's wrong?" Sofia asked.

"I'm not sure," Sam said. He opened the projector and removed the reel of film to take a closer look. A moment later, he shook his head sadly. "It looks like the film got wet. I think that's the end of your movie, Aunt Charlie."

"Isn't there something we can do?" Sofia asked hopefully. She loved solving problems. Creative solutions were her specialty.

"I'm afraid not," Aunt Charlie said, walking up to the projector. "It's almost impossible to save film damaged by water. What a shame." She looked disappointed. "But I suppose that can happen with twenty-year-old film."

"I'm sorry," Sam said to his aunt. "I wish Sofia and I could fix it."

"Thank you both," Aunt Charlie said, holding up the stained filmstrip, "but the only way to fix this would be to go to Egypt and shoot more footage."

Sam shot Sofia an excited glance.

"No sense in wallowing, though," Aunt Charlie said. "Looks like you kids are off the hook until tonight. I need to go over my notes and make some changes, and I'm sure you two have better things to do than wait around."

She seemed to cheer up slightly as she lifted her thick folder of Egyptian research notes.

"You two enjoy the afternoon," she said. "Just don't be late for the show-and-tell tonight. I need my team here to run the lights and operate the popcorn machine. We can't have a community event without snacks!"

"Of course!" Sam said, a bit louder than he needed to. "See you tonight, Aunt Charlie."

Sam turned to Sofia as Aunt Charlie headed out of the theater.

"I have a *super* idea," he said. "Come on!"

The pair headed out the front door of the community center and down the block, walking fast.

"Are we going where I think we're going?" Sofia asked.

Sam nodded.

"Aunt Charlie's lab," he replied, and the two of them hurried up the walkway to Sam's house, where he lived with his aunt. A few more steps to the back door, and they were in the garage. Aunt Charlie had transformed the space into a laboratory filled with all of her high-tech scientific gadgets and incredible inventions.

Once inside, Sam pulled out a stepladder. He climbed up and began rummaging around a shelf full of microscopes, test tubes, and other equipment. "I know it's up here somewhere."

"What's up there somewhere?" Sofia asked excitedly. "What are you looking for?"

"Almost . . . got it!" Sam cried. He pulled a dusty box off the shelf and brushed off the top. He stepped down and removed the lid carefully, revealing a small handheld movie camera.

"Is that a . . ." Sofia began.

"A Super 8?" Sam finished her question. "Sure

is! I knew Aunt Charlie still had it. Now all we need is film."

Sam headed for the refrigerator in the corner of the garage. It was where Aunt Charlie kept her favorite drinks and snacks.

"Um, are you hungry?" Sofia asked.

Sam opened the door and rummaged around. A second later, he popped up, a box of Super 8 film in his hand.

"If you mean *hungry* for an adventure!" he joked.

Sofia raised her eyebrows. "Why does Aunt Charlie keep film in the fridge?" she asked.

"Unused film like this has to be stored at a cool temperature," Sam explained. "The fridge is the best place."

He put the camera and the film in his messenger bag and turned to Sofia.

"Ready to hear my idea?" he asked.

"Only if it includes *that*," Sofia said, pointing

toward a large tarp-covered object in the corner of the lab.

"Bingo!" Sam said, a huge smile on his face.

He strode over to the tarp and pulled it off with a **whoosh**. The cover fell away to reveal a candy-apple-red scooter that shone brightly, as if beckoning them to climb on. Sam ran his hand over the sleek machine. Both Sofia and Sam knew it had the power to transport its riders anywhere on the globe in an instant. They had already used it to travel to Brazil and some other countries.

"If we reshoot Aunt Charlie's damaged footage with the Super 8, she'll have everything she needs for tonight's show-and-tell," Sam said. "What do you say?"

"I say it's time for a trip to Egypt," Sofia replied, her voice bubbling with excitement.

Sam smiled and hopped on the scooter. He tapped the touch screen on the handlebars as

13

Sofia got on behind him.

The screen lit up and a spinning globe appeared. Yellow letters danced by.

Sam typed the answer: **THE TEMPLE OF KOM OMBO, EGYPT**

The globe zoomed in to a closer view of Egypt, and a flashing dot appeared in the southeastern part of the country, near a winding blue line labeled "Nile River."

"Ready?" Sam asked, his finger hovering over the green button that had appeared on the screen.

"*Vamos!*" Sofia replied.

Sam tapped the button and, instantly, the headlights, taillights, and touch screen glowed brightly inside the small garage. A radiant, glittering orb surrounded the scooter. It quickly became too bright for Sam to keep his eyes open. He squeezed them shut and gripped the handlebars tight.

"Hang on," he said. "Here we go!"

Whiz ... Zoom ... Foop!

3

Ancient Ruins

When Sam opened his eyes, the walls and gadget-filled shelves of Aunt Charlie's lab had disappeared. The scooter was standing on the side of a hot, dusty road in what looked like a desert. Sam's stomach felt as though he had just ridden the world's fastest rollercoaster. He climbed off the scooter slowly, giving his legs a second to stop trembling. No matter how many times he and Sofia used the scooter, it was thrilling each time.

Sam looked around. On one side of the road, barren desert stretched as far as he could see. On the other side, there was a cluster of palm trees and some green shrubs. Just past those, Sam saw a wide, dark river. It was much, much bigger than the creek near Compass Court, where he liked to sit and draw pictures of the local wildlife. A few small boats floated lazily on the smooth water.

"Is that the Nile?" Sofia whispered in awe.

"I think so," Sam replied. "And look!"

He shielded his eyes from the bright orange sun and pointed at some ruins a few hundred yards away. A crumbling wall covered in hieroglyphics stood next to the remains of a cluster of giant stone columns.

"Incredible!" Sofia gasped. "That must be the Temple of Kom Ombo. Imagine what it must have looked like when it was first built."

"Let's get a closer look," Sam said. He parked the scooter near a group of motorbikes. Ahead, there was a small plaza in front of the temple. It was early in the day, and the area wasn't crowded. There were some locals roaming about and a few tourists taking photos in front of the magnificent ruins. Along with the Super 8, Sam had brought his own camera, which he pulled from his bag and pointed toward the temple.

Click-click! Click-click!

Sofia took a small notebook and pencil from her pocket.

"I'll make a list of all the film footage we need to get while we're here," she said. "Okay, first there is the ancient Egyptian calendar in hieroglyphics. Aunt Charlie said that's somewhere here in the temple."

Sofia scribbled in her notebook.

"She also mentioned a crocodile mummy," Sam said, "but I don't know where we would find that."

Sofia nodded and added it to her list.

"Finally, she talked about an archaeological dig," Sofia added. She made one more note and tapped the pencil against the notebook thoughtfully. "I guess we should start with the calendar, since we know it's close by."

"Good plan," Sam agreed. He turned and started toward the temple, determination in each step. Just ahead, a woman in a pink scarf was leading a group of tourists.

"This temple is unique because it was devoted to two Egyptian gods rather than one," the guide said, her voice echoing in the nearly empty plaza. "The left side was dedicated to Horus, the sky god, and the right side honors the crocodile god, Sobek."

"Let's follow her," Sofia said softly. "Maybe she'll lead us to the calendar."

Sam nodded.

"I feel like Courageous Cecilia Crosby on one of her missions," Sam whispered to Sofia as they fell back, trailing the group. Sam lifted his bag and swapped his camera for the Super 8, excited to try it out.

"Now we're entering the temple's hypostyle

hall, which honored both of the two gods," the guide went on. Sam and Sofia looked up in wonder at the enormous hieroglyphic-covered columns that filled the space.

"I wonder what a *hippo-style* hall is," Sofia whispered curiously. "Do you see hippos in these hieroglyphics?"

"Courageous Crosby visits one in my comic," Sam said eagerly. "It's spelled H-Y-P-O-S-T-Y-L-E. All Egyptian temples have one. It's a large dark room with light coming in through one small window in the center of the roof. The only people allowed in the room were the most important priests or the pharaoh himself."

"Wow," Sofia said softly, craning her neck to get a better look. "Incredible!"

" . . . follow me this way, and I'll show you a full ancient Egyptian calendar in hieroglyphics," the guide was saying.

"This is it, Sam!" Sofia said excitedly, poking

Sam. "*Vamos!*"

Sam and Sofia hurried after the guide. She led them to a corner where two sand-colored walls met. Though the surface was crumbling in places, the stone was covered in vivid, detailed hieroglyphic carvings.

"This is the only full calendar that remains today," the guide explained. "Other temples have calendars showing just a few months, but this is a complete year."

Sofia hopped excitedly from one foot to the other as Sam raised the camera to get the footage. He took a breath, pressed the button to begin recording and . . . nothing happened.

"Ugh," he groaned. "It's not working!"

Sam popped open the battery compartment.

"I can't believe it!" he cried, smacking his forehead in dismay. He held out the camera, showing it to Sofia. "I forgot the batteries!"

4

Mummies at the Museum

ofia jumped into problem-solving mode. "Okay, what type of batteries does the camera take?" she asked.

Sam studied the Super 8 for a second.

"Hmm . . . looks like double-A."

"Great," Sofia replied. "Those are the easiest to find. Now we need a shop."

Sam looked around, but all he saw were the temple ruins, a few palm trees, and the Nile in the distance.

"Over there!" Sofia said suddenly. She pointed at a sign near the entrance to the ruins. It read **Crocodile Museum** with a large arrow pointing the way.

"That must be where Aunt Charlie saw the crocodile mummies!" Sam said.

Sofia nodded, her eyes dancing happily. "And it might have a gift shop that sells batteries."

"Let's find out," Sam said. He and Sofia followed the arrow, walking along a flat stone path. Soon a squat brick building came into view. The Sun was higher in the sky now, and the dry air was growing hotter by the minute. When Sofia opened the door to the museum, she and Sam were blasted with a rush of cool air.

Sam hurried inside behind her, tiny goosebumps popping up all over his arms and legs from the air conditioning. In front of them was a ticket desk, and to the left was a gift stand.

"Yes!" Sofia exclaimed, and she and Sam hurried over.

"*Ahlan wa sahlan*," said the man behind the counter. "Welcome. How can I help you?"

"We're looking for double-A batteries for my camera," Sam said. He showed the man the empty compartment of his Super 8.

"Of course," the man replied. He pulled some batteries off a rack and passed them to Sofia. "That will be eighty pounds."

"How much is that in US dollars?" Sam asked.

"Egyptian currency is a bit different from yours, isn't it?" The man smiled kindly. "Eighty pounds is about five dollars."

Sam rummaged around in his messenger bag as Sofia searched her pockets. They looked at each other, a pit forming in Sam's stomach.

"Sam," Sofia whispered. "What are we gonna do? We don't have any—"

Suddenly, a harried-looking woman rounded a corner and slammed right into Sam, knocking the camera out of his hands. The woman's bag also went flying.

"*Ya msebty!*" she exclaimed in surprise. "I'm so sorry!"

She scrambled to pick up the camera, handing it back to Sam.

"Did I break it?" she asked worriedly.

He looked over the camera quickly, but it looked fine. "It's okay," Sam replied.

Sofia bent down to collect the items that had spilled out of the woman's bag. There was a pen, an eyeglass case, a handful of papers, and a small blue felt bag with an unusual beetle symbol stamped on it in gold ink.

"What's that?" Sam asked, but the woman quickly grabbed the small bag from Sofia.

"Oh, that's nothing," she said, stuffing it back into her bag. "Are you sure the camera is okay?"

"It will be fine as soon as we get those," Sam said, nodding to the batteries Sofia was holding.

"Do you still want them?" the man asked.

"We do," Sofia said, "but we don't have any money."

The woman pulled a handful of bills out of her pocket and pressed them into Sam's hand. As she did, he noticed the same beetle design on the pocket of her shirt.

"Here," she said apologetically. "I'm sorry I was in such a hurry. I'm glad your camera didn't break."

"Wow!" Sam said in surprise. "Thanks so much. You don't have to—"

But the woman had already rushed off.

"How strange," Sam muttered. But he quickly turned back to the man at the counter and handed him the money.

"*Shukran*," the clerk replied. "Thank you. Enjoy your time in Egypt!"

"Thank you!" Sam said. Then he popped the batteries in and turned on the Super 8.

Click-whirr-whirr!

"Yes! It works!" Sam said happily.

"Great," Sofia said. "Now let's find those mummies."

She headed in the same direction the hurrying woman had gone.

"Did you see that little blue bag that woman dropped?" Sam asked, following Sofia. "The beetle symbol was on her shirt too."

"Maybe it's a sign of good luck?" Sofia said. "It was pretty lucky that she gave us the money for the batteries, right?"

"True," Sam said, smiling as a glass display

case caught his eye. "Look! The mummies!"

"Amazing," Sofia said softly as the two walked over. She peered at the five crocodile mummies inside the case. They were unwrapped and dark brown in color. Each mummy was so detailed you could see the crocodile's teeth and the scales on its skin.

"I can't believe these are more than two thousand years old," Sofia said. "Look! That one even has tiny baby crocodiles on its back."

"Whoa," Sam breathed. "Time to get some footage."

He turned on the Super 8 camera, raised it to his eye, and pressed the button to record.

Click-whirr-whirr!

But just as Sam pointed the lens of the camera at the crocodile mummies, the museum lights flickered and went out.

5

Lights Out!

"Uh, Sam?" Sofia called out. "What's happening?"

"I don't know," Sam replied. It was so dark he could barely make out his own hand holding the camera in front of him. "But I didn't get any footage. Can you see anything?"

"Not a thing," Sofia said from his right.

Sam took a step toward her, but his toe hit something bulky.

"Ouch!" he cried out.

"Wait a minute," Sofia said. "I think I have something that will help."

Sam heard Sofia fiddling around in the dark. She always carried unusual odds and ends in her pockets and was a pro at using these gadgets in sticky situations.

"Yes!" Sofia exclaimed. "Here we go."

A thin beam of light cut through the darkness as Sofia pointed a keychain flashlight at Sam.

"Nice find," Sam said, relieved. His eyes followed the light, which danced around the gallery.

Sofia looked around in the dark. "Do you know which direction we came from?"

Sam shook his head. He had been so excited

to see the crocodiles that he hadn't been paying attention. The light landed on one of the mummies, and Sam took a step toward the display case.

"It looks even cooler in the dark," he said.

Sofia moved the light from one crocodile to the next. "Uh, Sam? Weren't there five mummies in this case?"

Sam pictured the case in his mind. "Yeah," he said, "definitely five."

"But now there are only . . . one, two, three, four!" Sofia said.

Sam pulled out his comic book with a gasp.

"Sofia, something just like this happens in *Courageous Crosby's Hunt for the Lost Pyramid*!" he said.

He flipped the book open. Sofia shined the flashlight on the pages, which showed the adventurer Cecilia Crosby exploring an ancient Egyptian tomb.

"Crosby finds an urn covered in hieroglyphics," Sam explained. "It's a clue to the location of the lost pyramid, and she's about to translate the text when her lamp goes out. By the time Crosby relights the lamp, the urn is gone!"

"Spooky," Sofia whispered. "What happens after the urn goes missing?"

Sam heard a noise to their left. "Ah!" he yelped, startled.

Sofia swung the flashlight around.

"Hello?" she called out.

There was no reply.

"Come on," Sofia said to Sam. "Let's figure out how to get out of here."

Sam followed Sofia slowly through the gallery. He stayed close to her as she moved carefully through the room, swinging the light left to right. Partway through the exhibit, Sam stumbled in the dark and bumped into Sofia.

"Whoops," he said sheepishly. "Sorry."

"That's okay," Sofia said, pointing the keychain down to see if Sam had tripped over something. As the beam of light moved, Sam saw the doorway that led to the rest of the museum.

"There!" he said, pointing. "The exit must be that way."

Sam took a step forward and, out of the corner of his eye, saw something move in the dark.

"Sofia?" he whispered.

"Did you see that?"

"What?" Sofia asked. She moved the flashlight to the doorway, the beam landing near a dark figure standing in the shadows.

"Sam?" Sofia asked.

"Yeah?" Sam said.

"What happened to the urn Cecilia Crosby found in your comic book?"

"A thief took it," Sam said quietly. "Do you think that's a thief, too?"

"There's only one way to find out," Sofia replied. Then she cleared her throat and raised her voice. "Who's there?"

They waited a moment in silence, and then the figure stepped forward.

6

Thief on the Loose

A boy about their age was illuminated by Sofia's flashlight.

"Hi," he said. "You two okay?" He smiled warmly. "I'm Tarek."

"Oh, hi," Sam replied, his heart still racing.

"I'm Sam, and this is Sofia."

"We're just a little turned around," Sofia said as Tarek walked over. "You startled us."

Sofia stuck out her hand and Tarek shook it, his face open and friendly.

"I didn't mean to scare you," he said, shaking Sam's hand too. "I saw your light across the room. I wanted to make sure you were okay. I know my way around here pretty well. I come here a lot."

"With your school?" Sofia asked.

"No," Tarek replied, smiling again. "My father is an archaeologist. Some of his discoveries are on display here. He's actually working on an excavation site nearby."

"What a relief," Sam said. "We think there might be a thief in the museum."

"A thief?" Tarek asked.

"When the lights went out, it reminded me of a scene in my comic book," Sam explained.

He showed Tarek his copy of the Courageous Crosby story. "A thief steals an urn from her when the flame on her lamp goes out."

Tarek raised both of his eyebrows in surprise.

Sofia pointed at the crocodile mummy display a few steps behind them.

"And before it went dark, there were five mummies in that case," she said.

"Hmm," Tarek said, walking over to study the display. "And there are only four now."

"Exactly," Sofia replied. Her face was serious.

"We think someone stole the fifth mummy when it went dark," Sam explained.

"Strange," Tarek said thoughtfully. "That's not the only thing that's gone missing lately."

"Really?" Sam asked.

Tarek nodded in the shadows. "Yesterday, a priceless carving of a cat disappeared from the dig where my father is working."

Sam's eyes widened in surprise. "Maybe there really is a thief on the loose, just like in my comic."

Tarek nodded. "It's possible."

"But we don't have any proof," Sofia said slowly.

"And there's not much we can do here in the museum," Tarek said, "especially in the dark. Come, let's get out of here."

Sam and Sofia followed Tarek as he led them through the dark rooms and back outside into the warm sunlight.

"I should let my dad know about the missing mummy," Tarek said. "He's back at the dig. Will you come and tell him what you saw?"

"Of course," Sofia said. "We'd love to visit the excavation site."

Sam smiled brightly. "Maybe we can get some

footage, too," he added.

"Footage?" Tarek asked.

Sam showed Tarek the Super 8 camera as Sofia took out her notebook and pencil.

"We're working on a film," Sam began.

"And we still need these three shots," Sofia explained, showing Tarek her notebook.

"I'm sure my father will let you film at the dig," he said.

"Great!" Sam said. "Lead the way."

"It's a pretty long walk," he said. "And hot. And there's only room for one person on my scooter."

Sam and Sofia looked at each other.

"Did you say scooter?" Sofia asked, smiling.

"Yes. I borrow it from my dad sometimes to get around town," Tarek said.

"That's incredible," Sam said, laughing. "We have a scooter too! It's parked over there."

He pointed toward the temple.

"Oh, perfect!" Tarek said, looking relieved.

"Mine's probably near yours. Follow me."

Sure enough, Tarek headed to the spot where Sam and Sofia had left Aunt Charlie's red scooter. Sam and Sofia climbed on while Tarek hopped onto his own, which looked a lot like theirs but was smaller and bright blue.

"We've never met someone who has a scooter like us," Sam said.

"A lot of people use them to get around here," said Tarek. "Just follow me!"

Sscrrreech!

"Here we go," Sam said to Sofia as he twisted the scooter's handle and followed Tarek away from the museum. The red scooter skidded along the road, the engine puttering smoothly.

"There's the Nile River," Tarek called out,

pointing at the sparkling blue waterway.

Sam could feel a gentle breeze coming off the water.

"This way," Tarek called. He turned off the smooth path onto a narrow, unmarked dirt road. "Sorry for the rough ride, but we'll get there faster."

Sure enough, the road was a bumpy one. The red scooter lurched over the rocky, uneven terrain, which climbed up one hill after another.

"Whoa!" Sam called out to Sofia. "Hold on!"

He tried his best to keep up with Tarek, but

with just one rider, the blue scooter was lighter and quicker than the red one. As the distance between the scooters grew, an alarm sounded in front of Sam.

Beep, beep, beep, beep, beep!

"Uh, Sam?" Sofia asked. "What's going on?"

Putt . . . putt . . . p-p-putt . . . putt . . . putt . . .

The engine sputtered.

"I'm not sure," Sam replied. He glanced at the touch screen and saw a flashing light. A moment later, the scooter came to a complete stop.

7

Scooter Shutdown

Sam and Sofia hopped off and exchanged a worried glance.

"Tarek!" Sam called out. "Hold up a second!"

Tarek quickly turned around and rode back to Sam and Sofia.

"Is everything okay?" he asked.

"I'm not sure," Sam replied.

"Maybe it's a quick fix," Sofia said hopefully.

Sam looked at the touch screen.

Sofia sighed. "Not a quick fix," she said, her shoulders slumping.

"Maybe we should move it to a shady spot while it cools," Sam said, looking to a small grove of trees near the side of the road. The three of them worked together to move the scooter into the shade. Sam glanced at his watch.

"We can't wait an hour before we get the

footage we need," he said, looking at Sofia meaningfully. "We need to be back for Aunt Charlie's presentation. Plus, we should tell your dad about the missing mummy as soon as possible," he added to Tarek.

But Tarek was looking past them to the Nile River, which they could see clearly from the top of the hill.

"I know!" he said. "We'll take a *felucca*!"

"Okay!" Sofia said with excitement. Then she tilted her head. "But what's a *felucca*?"

"I'll show you," Tarek said happily as they walked down the hill toward a small river dock.

When they reached the river, a small red-and-white boat with a large white sail was floating toward them. "That's a *felucca*," Tarek said, and he grinned when he saw the captain.

"How lucky!" Tarek told Sam and Sofia. "I know him." Tarek waved to the man and called, "Mostafa! *Izayyak?* These are my friends, Sam

and Sofia."

"Nice to meet you." Mostafa greeted them with a warm smile. "Any friends of Tarek are friends of mine."

"Mostafa cruises the Nile taking tourists to see the sites," Tarek told Sam and Sofia. "One of our scooters overheated. Can we get a ride to the excavation site? I'm seeing my father there."

"Of course," Mostafa replied, waving them aboard. "*Ahlan wa sahlan!*"

"Thank you," Sam said. He and Sofia followed Tarek across a plank that ran from the dock to the deck of the boat. Then they took their seats on some brightly colored pillows in the shade of a fabric canopy.

The *felucca* set sail, and Sam and Sofia sat back and relaxed for a moment.

"Can you believe we're sailing on the Nile River?" Sofia asked, amazed.

Sam shook his head as he reached into his

bag and pulled out the Super 8. He wanted to film the dark water and the bright green trees that lined the shore. He held the camera up to his right eye and peered through the viewfinder. Then he pressed the button to begin recording.

Click-whirr-whirr!

Sam loved the sound the camera made. It was so distinct, and it caused a little vibration in his hand as he filmed.

"Look to the left," Mostafa said, pointing to a bird floating on the water. "That's an Egyptian goose. The ancient Egyptians considered them to be sacred animals and painted them in much of their art."

The light-colored bird had a dark brown patch of feathers encircling its eye. Sam captured the bird on film before swinging the camera around to film the other passengers on the boat. There was a man in a long white tunic and a woman in the corner wearing a floppy sun hat. Once he

 had filmed for a few minutes, he decided to put the camera away and enjoy the rest of the ride. The breeze pushed the boat along quickly through the water, gently ruffling Sam's hair. He put his feet up and leaned back against one of the comfy cushions, closing his eyes.

Sam must have dozed off, because after what seemed like just a few seconds, Sofia gave him a gentle nudge.

"We're almost there," Tarek was telling them as he pointed toward shore. "We'll get off at that dock. The excavation site isn't far away."

As the boat pulled closer to the riverbank, the wind began to pick up, whipping Sam's hair into his eyes. Suddenly, a huge gust caught the hat of the woman sitting in the corner.

"*Ya msebty!*" she cried out as the hat flew off her head and into the water below.

"That's too bad," Sofia said sympathetically as she watched the woman's hat float away.

But Sam was more focused on the beetle design on her shirt.

"That's her!" he whispered with excitement. "That's the woman who bumped into me back at the museum shop!"

8

The Suspicious Scarab

Tarek looked puzzled.

"What woman?" he asked as the wind continued to whip around them.

"Before the lights went out at the museum, someone crashed into me when we were shopping for batteries," Sam said as gritty sand swirled through the hot air. "She was in a huge hurry, and she said the same thing when she bumped into me—*ya msebty.*"

"*Ya msebty* is a pretty common phrase here in Egypt," Tarek said. "It means 'oh my calamity' and is said like 'oh no' or 'oh dear' in English. Are you sure it's the same woman?"

"I'm sure," Sam said.

"I remember the beetle on her shirt!" Sofia added.

Tarek glanced over his shoulder at the woman. "That's a scarab," he explained. "They're also called dung beetles because they roll their dung into balls."

"Really?!" Sofia asked, fascinated.

"Look!" Sam said in a hushed voice. "There's a scarab beetle design on that crate, too."

Sofia and Tarek turned. The boat had reached the shore, and the woman was stepping onto the dock. As the kids watched, Mostafa lifted a small wooden crate from the deck of the boat and passed it to the woman. The wind blew the colorful canopy stretched above the passengers,

obscuring their view, but Sam glimpsed the painted scarab design. The woman grabbed the crate from Mostafa and hurried off.

"Isn't that crate about the same size as the crocodile mummy that went missing?" Sam asked. He had to speak loudly over the wind.

"It is!" Sofia exclaimed. "What if she's a thief, like in your comic?"

Sam wondered what Courageous Crosby would do. "Come on," he said. "Let's follow her!"

He hurried to the other end of the boat, the sandy wind lashing at his face. The man in the long tunic was climbing off the boat. He was carrying a large basket of fruit, and it took him a moment to disembark.

"Ouch!" Sam said as he scrambled off the boat after the fruit seller. "This sand really stings."

Sam tried to keep the woman in sight, but he had to keep glancing down at the ground to keep the sand out of his eyes.

Tarek pointed at the dark, hazy sky.

"It's a *khamasin*," he explained. "It's a hot wind that causes a sandstorm. They usually only last about thirty minutes, luckily."

On the dock, people began hurrying inside nearby buildings to get out of the storm.

Sam squinted through the sand, trying to find the woman in the scarab beetle shirt in the crowd. But the woman was nowhere to be seen.

"Oh no," Sam groaned. "I lost her!"

9

A Taste of Egypt

Tarek and Sofia caught up with Sam.

"Let's get out of this wind," Tarek said quickly. "Follow me."

He dashed under a striped awning and inside a small building. As Sam followed, he noticed a sign over the door that read *El Tayn Café*.

Once he set foot inside, Sam was enveloped by a warm, spicy aroma. He brushed some sand from his clothes and checked to make sure the Super 8's lens hadn't been scratched in the storm.

"Mmm," Sofia said. "That smells absolutely wonderful. I haven't eaten since breakfast, and that was ages ago."

Tarek grinned. "This place has the best falafel," he said. "How about some lunch?"

Sam tucked the camera safely into his bag. "Yes, please," he replied eagerly. He hadn't realized how hungry he was until he smelled the delicious scent of food cooking.

"I love falafel," Sofia added as she and Sam sat down at a small table near the door. "It's one of my favorites back home in the United States."

"You've probably had the kind made from chickpeas," Tarek explained. "In Egypt, we use fava beans. It's delicious. I'll order for all of us."

Tarek headed straight for the counter near the small open kitchen. When he returned a few minutes later, he was juggling four plates of food.

Sofia jumped up to grab one before it fell.

"I got us each a falafel sandwich," Tarek announced. "It's served on pita bread with tomato, onions, and tahini sauce. And I also ordered *koshari* for us to share. You can't visit Egypt without trying some. It's my favorite."

Sam's stomach rumbled loudly, and he smiled sheepishly.

"*Koshari*?" he asked. "What's that?"

"It's lentils, rice, and macaroni that's covered in spicy tomato sauce and topped with chickpeas and fried onions," Tarek said. "Try it!"

Sam and Sofia each had a bite of the colorful dish.

"That's so yummy!" Sofia said.

"I told you," Tarek said with a smile.

Sam and Sofia tucked into their lunch. As Sam ate, he thought about the woman in the scarab shirt again.

"Do you really think the woman from the museum stole the crocodile mummy?" he wondered aloud to Tarek and Sofia.

Sofia shrugged. "Anything's possible," she said. "But she also helped us get the batteries for your camera. Doesn't seem like something a thief would do. "

"True," Sam said thoughtfully. "But if she is a thief, she's even closer to the excavation site now."

"As soon as we get to the dig," Tarek said, "we can warn my—*Baba!*"

Tarek dropped his fork in surprise and jumped up from the table. Sam and Sofia turned to see a tall man who had just stepped into the café, bringing a blast of hot, sandy air with him.

"Tarek," the man said, grinning broadly and

pulling Tarek into a hug.

"This is my father," Tarek said. "*Baba*, these are my new friends, Sam and Sofia."

"I'm Khalil. It's a pleasure to meet you both," Tarek's father said kindly. "I'm here to pick up lunch for my crew at the dig."

"That's where we were heading," Tarek said eagerly. "We just stopped to get out of the storm and have some lunch."

"Wonderful," Khalil said, smiling as he tousled Tarek's hair. "Amir is there now. I'm sure he would be happy to give Sam and Sofia a tour of the site. I wish I could do it myself, but my schedule is packed today."

"I know, *Baba*," Tarek said. "Do you have a minute, though? I have to tell you something import—"

Khalil's phone buzzed loudly. He glanced down to read a message.

"I'm so sorry," he said. "This looks urgent. I have to run off—oh, but the food!"

Khalil seemed flustered.

"Maybe we can bring lunch to the crew?" Sofia offered.

"We are heading to the site anyway," Tarek agreed.

"Wonderful, wonderful!" Khalil exclaimed, looking relieved. He squeezed Tarek's shoulder. "Looks like your friends are as helpful as you are, son. Thank you! And we'll talk more when I get back to the site, I promise."

Khalil opened the door of the café, and the sound of the wind rushed in.

"But, *Baba*," Tarek called over the storm, "I have to tell you something really quickly—"

But the whipping air was too loud, and with a slap of the door, Khalil was gone.

10

Discovery at the Dig

arek, Sam, and Sofia waited for the food. Once it was ready, they each grabbed a bag and headed outside. It was still incredibly hot, but the wind was much calmer.

Tarek led the way down an unpaved road that

was lined with small shrubs. Sam was quiet as he thought about the missing mummy and the woman from both the museum and the boat. As he walked with Tarek and Sofia, he also realized they still hadn't taken a single shot they needed for Aunt Charlie's film. Would they have enough time, or would they have to return to Compass Court empty handed?

He sighed, feeling frustrated.

"It's not much farther," Tarek reassured him. He pointed to a sign about a hundred feet ahead. "That's the turnoff."

When they reached the sign, Tarek, Sam, and Sofia turned to the right. The road here wasn't paved, but there were two well-marked parallel ruts that Sam could tell had been formed by vehicles traveling to and from the site.

"Here we are!" Tarek said. The site was about the size of the playground back at Compass Community Center. It looked like the remains of a temple or another structure, with rows of troughs and walls dug into the earth. Not far from Sam and Sofia, about half a dozen workers were crouching or kneeling in one of the troughs. They were carefully using what looked like small knives and brushes to gently remove dirt from a mostly buried stone.

"Hey, Tarek!" a young man called out. He put down his tools and headed over to where Sam, Sofia, and Tarek were standing.

"Hi, Amir," Tarek greeted him. He held up the bag of food. "Lunch is here!"

At that moment, the group of people working nearby began chattering excitedly. They were huddled around one of the many patches of dry earth.

Tarek's eyes lit up. He turned to Sam and Sofia.

"Come on!" he said. "Looks like Sarah has found something."

Sam and Sofia exchanged an eager glance

before following Tarek and Amir toward the cluster of archaeologists, lunch momentarily forgotten.

Sam pulled out the Super 8 and began recording.

Click-whirr-whirr!

A woman in dirt-speckled clothes showed Amir and the others her find. It looked like a dusty stone about the size of a quarter. As she brushed it off and held it out for everyone to see more closely, Sofia gasped.

"It's a scarab!" she said softly.

"Like the one on the mysterious woman's shirt," Sam whispered. He stepped closer to get a better shot.

"Incredible find, Sarah," Amir told the archaeologist. "I haven't seen an intact piece like this in years."

He motioned for Tarek, Sam, and Sofia to come closer.

"I'm sure your friends would love to see this," he told Tarek. "It's a heart scarab amulet. It looks like it's carved from a type of stone called basalt. This would have been placed over the heart of a mummy for protection."

"Wow," Sam said in amazement. He could hardly believe he had captured the discovery on film!

"I feel like Courageous Crosby looking at a long-lost treasure," Sofia breathed as she whipped out her notebook and checked *archaeological dig* off their list of shots.

Sam kept filming as Sarah told the group all about the significance of the scarab beetle.

"Ancient Egyptians believed Khepri, god of the rising Sun, pushed the Sun across the sky each day," Sarah said. "When people saw scarab beetles pushing balls of dung around, the beetle became a symbol of renewal and rebirth, just like the god Khepri."

Sam captured footage of all the tools and supplies around the spot where the discovery had been made.

"The scarab beetle is still significant today," Sarah continued. "It even appears in the modern logo for the Treasures of the Nile Museum outside Cairo . . ."

Sam refocused the lens of the Super 8, gasped, and almost dropped the camera.

"Sofia! Tarek!" Sam sputtered, pulling his friends aside. He pointed across the excavation site. "Look! It's her!"

11

Power Play

On the far side of the excavation site, someone was loading crates into a dark blue van. It was the woman from the crocodile museum and the boat!

"What should we do?" Sofia asked quickly.

"Let's get a closer look," Tarek suggested.

"We have to hurry," Sam said. He tucked the Super 8 inside his messenger bag. "We can't let her get away again!"

"This way," Tarek said, leading them to the edge of the site. "We have to go around the troughs where people are working. This way should be fastest. "

Sam and Sofia scrambled after Tarek. They skirted the outside area of the dig and quickly found themselves in a vast meadow that a group of kids was using as a soccer field. A few rocks on the ground marked makeshift goalposts at either end.

Tarek tried to dash around the outside of the game, but one of the boys kicked the ball right toward him.

"Hey!" the kid yelled. "Kick it here!"

Tarek passed the ball back to him and kept jogging across the field. The boy hustled to the ball and then passed it to Sofia, who was quick on her feet. She sprinted a bit and nudged the ball toward another boy, who was getting close to the goal at the opposite end of the field.

"Here you go!" she called with a friendly wave.

"Sorry, we're in a hurry," Tarek called to the kids. "We can't play!"

Now Sam, Sofia, and Tarek were right near the goal, and the players kept kicking the ball in their direction. Up ahead, Sam could see the woman loading the last few crates into the back of the van.

"Take the shot!" one of the players shouted. With a skillful pass, he kicked the ball to Sam!

"Go for it, Sam!" Tarek called, looking back.

Sam sprinted a few steps and launched the ball forward with a powerful kick. It sailed right between the rocks marking the goal.

"He scores!" Sofia called, and the players cheered.

Sam laughed, but there wasn't much time to celebrate. They were now on the other side of the field, and the woman was almost finished loading the van.

"We have to hurry," Sam called to Sofia and Tarek.

"Who's that?" he heard Sofia ask.

And that's when Sam saw another person helping the mysterious woman. The man lifted the final crate as Tarek, Sam, and Sofia reached the van. He was about to close the side door when Sam saw who it was. His jaw dropped open.

"It can't be!" Tarek cried out in shock.

12

A Comic Mix-Up

It was Tarek's father. He looked up in surprise at the three of them as they skidded to a stop in front of the van.

"Hi!" he said with a friendly smile to Sam and Sofia. "Nice to see you two again." Then he turned back to Tarek. "Did you drop off the lunches?"

"Yes. But what are you doing?" Tarek asked.

Sam eyed the woman suspiciously as she closed her bag.

"I'm loading some crates into this van," Tarek's father replied with a chuckle. "That's pretty obvious, isn't it?"

Sam craned his neck to peer inside the van. Crates and boxes were stacked up, filling the space. The van was crammed full, but then Sam spotted it.

 "There it is!" Sam said, pointing at the crate marked with the scarab design. "What's inside that one right there?"

The woman glanced at her watch and tapped her foot impatiently.

"Khalil, what's this about?" she asked. "I really

have to go."

"Of course," Khalil said. "Kids, this is my friend, Nour."

"Yes, hello," she said with a quick smile.

"Would you mind showing us what's in that crate really quickly?" Tarek asked his father. "Please?"

"If Nour doesn't mind, that is," Sofia added.

Khalil sighed. "She is in a rush, you know."

"A big one, yes," Nour added. "But yes, okay. If it means that much to you."

Sam instinctively pulled out his Super 8 and began filming.

Click-whirr-whirr!

Khalil carefully slid the crate out of the van and opened it to reveal the crocodile mummy from the museum.

Sofia gasped. "It's true!" she said, turning to Nour. "You really *did* take the mummy from the museum!"

Tarek looked pale and anxious.

"*Baba*," he said softly, "What's going on?"

"You tell me," Khalil said.

"Is there a problem?" Nour asked.

Tarek's father looked from his son to Sam and Sofia.

Sofia stepped up to explain. "We saw Nour at the crocodile museum earlier today," she said. "Then a minute later, the lights went out, and this mummy went missing from the display. And now here it is!"

"I remember Nour because of the scarab on her shirt," Sam said, turning to face her. "I noticed it when you bumped into me," he explained. "And there's one on the crate here, too. See? The same type of scarab Sarah just told us about, actually, which is the logo for the Treasures of the Nile Museum."

Sam lowered his camera and looked from the crate to Nour. "Wait a minute . . ." he said slowly.

A look of sudden realization crossed Sofia's face. Her eyes widened and she looked at the woman sheepishly.

"You aren't a thief, are you?" Sam asked.

"A thief?" Nour laughed warmly. Khalil joined

her, letting out a chuckle of his own.

"No, I am certainly not," she said kindly. "Though if I were, it looks like I wouldn't have gotten far with you three around."

"Nour works for the Treasures of the Nile Museum," Tarek's dad said. "She's trying to get back before the museum closes for the day."

"This crocodile mummy," Nour said, lifting the crate, "is going to be part of a new exhibition. I'm also showcasing some of the recent finds from the  excavation site here, including a statue of a cat."

Tarek looked relieved. "That explains things," he said sheepishly.

Nour nodded. "That's why I'm in such a hurry," she explained, glancing at her watch again. Then she turned to Sam. "I'm sorry I bumped into you at the museum and rushed off. And I can understand why the blackout made everything more mysterious. Someone was trimming a tree outside, and a branch accidentally fell on one of the power lines."

Sam hung his head. It seemed there was a good explanation for everything that had happened.

"It was Nour who texted you when we were at the café, wasn't it, *Baba*?" Tarek asked.

Tarek's dad nodded. "She was running behind schedule, so she asked for help loading the van."

"Speaking of which, I really *do* need to go," Nour repeated.

Sam and Sofia exchanged a glance. Neither of them seemed ready to admit it, but they knew their time in Egypt had to end soon.

"We need to get home too," Sam said. "We're sorry for the misunderstanding."

"Yeah," Sofia added. "We really let our imaginations run wild, didn't we?"

"That's okay," Nour said. "It sounds like something out of a Cecilia Crosby story."

Sam gasped. "You read comics?" he asked.

"I love them!" Nour replied, laughing.

"Cecilia Crosby is one of my favorites," Sam said, amazed.

"I bet Courageous Crosby would be proud of how protective you three were of our incredible crocodile mummy," Nour said. "And you showed yourselves to be excellent detectives. In the end, you solved the mystery, right?"

Sam laughed. "That's true!"

"But don't you need a few more shots for your movie?" Tarek asked.

"Actually, I just got the crocodile mummy on film!" Sam said happily as he pointed to the crate in the back of the van.

Sofia pulled out her notebook and checked

her list. "And we already got the excavation site," she said. "The only one left is a shot of the hieroglyphic calendar at the Temple of Kom Ombo."

"Do we have time?" Sam asked her. "We need to get back to our scooter and make sure it's working again."

"Maybe I can help," Nour said.

13

One More Stop

"Really?" Sofia asked in surprise. "How?"

"I have to drive that way to get back to Cairo," Nour said. "If we leave now, I can drop you off at your scooter. Where is it?"

"I'm not exactly sure how to get back there,"

Sam said, retracing their steps in his mind.

"It's okay," Tarek jumped in. "I know where we parked the scooters. I can ride with you, and I'll navigate."

"Sounds good," Khalil agreed. "I'll see you back at home for dinner, Tarek."

"Thanks, *Baba*!" Tarek said happily. "Tell Sarah and Amir I'm sorry I ran off so quickly."

Khalil smiled and waved. "I will," he said.

Sam and Sofia said goodbye and squeezed into the van's back seat. Tarek sat in front so he could give directions. After a short ride, Tarek pointed to the two scooters up ahead.

"There they are!" he said. The scooters were right where they had left them, in the shade of the trees.

"Wait," Nour said before they could hop out of the car. "One last thing before you go."

She handed Sam, Sofia, and Tarek each a small bag.

The bags were stamped with the scarab icon in metallic gold ink.

Sam gasped when he saw the bags. He carefully opened it to find a scarab amulet on a silk cord inside.

"Wow!" Sofia murmured as she opened her bag and slipped the charm around her neck. Sam did the same, looping the amulet over his neck and feeling the scarab on his chest.

"They're from the museum," Nour explained. "As a special thank you for your dedication to Egyptian antiquities."

"Thanks so much!" Sam said.

He realized how wrong he had been about Nour. First she had bought batteries for his camera, and now she had given all three of them special souvenirs.

Sam hopped out of the car and headed toward the scooter. *Please let it work, please let it work*, he thought to himself as he tapped the scooter's touch screen. Sofia's forehead was creased with worry.

To Sam's great relief, the scooter powered up without trouble. The battery was at thirty percent, which would be plenty of power to get them home.

"It works!" Sam announced, a note of relief in his voice.

"Great!" Nour called from the driver's seat. "Enjoy the rest of your trip."

"Thanks again," Sofia replied. She, Sam, and Tarek waved as Nour's van pulled away and headed toward the highway to Cairo.

Tarek hopped on his blue scooter and said, "Follow me!"

Sofia took her seat as Sam twisted the handle, the engine leaping to life. A moment later, they were zipping down the dusty road toward the temple, the wind whipping across Sam's face as they flew downhill. After a few minutes, he saw the temple ahead.

The sun was beginning to sink on the horizon, and the crumbling columns seemed to glow in the rosy pink light.

Tarek led them back to the spot where Sam had parked Aunt Charlie's red scooter that morning. They parked the scooters again and hurried straight to the hieroglyphic calendar in the temple. Sam started filming with a huge smile.

"The lighting right now is perfect!" he said excitedly. "In photography, they call this the golden hour."

"Really?" Tarek asked. "Why?"

"Because right before sunset, the light has a soft golden color that makes everything look good—especially ancient Egyptian ruins," Sam explained. "This is going to look spectacular."

"Sam, that's it!" Sofia said as she pulled out her notebook and checked all the boxes on her list. "We got all the shots we needed for Aunt Charlie. First we got the amazing discovery at the archaeological site, then the mummy with Nour, and now the calendar!"

Film Footage

☑ Calendar in hieroglyphics

☑ Crocodile mummy

☑ Archaeological dig

"Thanks again for your help," Sam told Tarek as he put away the Super 8 and pulled out his still camera. "We couldn't have done all this without you."

"I hope you'll come visit again someday," Tarek said. "We can take a train to visit the Great Sphinx and the pyramids in Cairo."

Sam and Sofia both laughed.

"Now let's get a picture together," Sam said, turning the camera around for a selfie.

"Say cheese!" Sam said.

"Cheese sticks!" Sofia replied, laughing.

Click-click.

Tarek hopped on his scooter and turned back to them.

"Thanks again for a fantastic adventure," he called to Sam and Sofia. "Get home safely!"

Tarek waved as he pulled away and rode off in the golden light.

"We'd better hurry," Sofia said to Sam. "Aunt Charlie's talk is starting soon."

She and Sam hopped on the scooter. Sam tapped the screen and was again relieved when it started up.

"Time to go home," Sofia said.

Sam pressed the green button, and the warm glow of light from the scooter's headlamps and taillights lit up the dusty pink desert landscape around them.

"Hang on, Sofia!" Sam cried.

Whiz . . . Zoom . . . FOOP!

14
Lights, Camera, Action!

A moment later, Sam, Sofia, and the scooter were back in Aunt Charlie's lab.

Sam hopped off the scooter and shook out his legs, sprinkling some sand onto the floor.

"Whoops!" he said, smiling. "I'll have to sweep

that up later."

"Yes, later, Sam!" Sofia said urgently. "*Vamos!* Aunt Charlie's talk already started!"

"I have the film," Sam said, patting his messenger bag. "Let's do this!"

They headed outside and raced to Compass Community Center. Sofia pulled the door of the theater open slowly and quietly, hoping not to attract too much attention. She and Sam slipped into the back, which smelled of fresh popcorn and was dark and full of people.

"Whoops!" Sofia whispered. "Looks like we didn't make it back in time to make the snacks."

She glanced over at the popcorn machine, where her mother Lyla was busy scooping up bags of the buttery snack.

"Don't worry," Sam said. "The footage will make up for it."

He and Sofia hurried to the back of the room where the projector was set up. The first part of

Aunt Charlie's film was playing, and the crowd had just *oohed* and *ahhed* in delight at the footage from inside King Tut's tomb.

"Do you still have your flashlight?" Sam whispered to Sofia.

Sofia nodded and pulled out the light just as the reel of film cut to black. The crowd groaned with disappointment.

By the light of Sofia's flashlight, Sam pulled the Super 8 out of his bag, popped the new film out of the camera, and looped it into the projector. A moment later, his footage of the Nile River appeared on the screen. The crowd clapped and cheered.

Aunt Charlie looked up and saw Sam and Sofia standing at the projector. She smiled proudly, gave them a wink, and jumped right back into her talk.

"Here we are, back on the Nile River," Aunt Charlie said, smiling at Sam.

"This part of the film," Aunt Charlie said, "is a little different than I remember, but you know memories—they seem to change with time, don't they?"

Sam found two empty seats in a back row and slipped into one of them. Then he looked around for Sofia, who seemed to have disappeared. A second later, she sat down in the seat next to his and handed him a bag of popcorn for them to share.

Sam sat back and munched happily on a handful of warm, buttery popcorn. At that moment, the footage from the archaeological site appeared on the screen. The audience murmured in delight at the sight of the scarab amulet being unearthed. Sam held the amulet hanging around his neck, rubbed the scarab, and smiled happily as he enjoyed the show.

النهاية

(The End)

Arabic Terms

- **Baba** - Dad

- **El Tayn** - Fig

- **Felucca** - Traditional wooden sailboat

- **Khamasin** - Dust storm

- **Koshari** - Egyptian dish of rice, macaroni, and lentils, topped with tomato sauce

- **Shukran** - Thank you

Portuguese Terms

- **Papai** - Dad

- **Vamos!** - Let's go!

Arabic Phrases

- Ahlan wa sahlan! - Welcome!

- Izayyak? - How are you?

- Ya msebty! - Oh my calamity! / Oh dear!

Super 8 Film Facts

The small square hole on the left of each Super 8 film frame serves an important purpose. When the film is fed through a projector, a mechanism hooks into each of these holes and pulls the film in front of a shining light, which projects the image of each frame through a lens and onto a movie screen.

For a standard film, the images move past the lens at a rate of 24 frames per second!

Sofia and Sam's Snippets

Egypt was established in 3100 BCE. The country's capital city is Cairo, the official language spoken is Egyptian Arabic, and the currency used is the Egyptian pound.

Cairo

EGYPT

About 100 million people call Egypt home.

10 Egyptian pounds

1 Egyptian pound

Scarab beetles were honored by the ancient Egyptians as symbols of the sun god Khepri. In 2018, rare mummified scarabs were discovered in a series of tombs in Saqqara, about 20 miles south of Cairo.

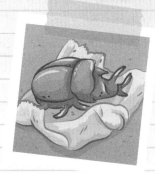

The Arabian camel has one hump and lives in Egypt and other desert areas of North Africa. The camel can convert the extra fat in its hump into energy when water and food are scarce in the dry environment.

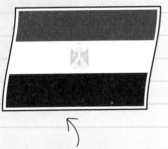

Egyptian flag

An Arabian camel can weigh as much as 1,600 pounds and can carry up to 80 pounds of fat in its hump.

Football

Football (called soccer in the United States) is the most popular sport in Egypt today. The Egyptian national team, The Pharaohs, won the Africa Cup of Nations in 2006, 2008, and 2010.

The Pyramids at Giza were built more than 4,500 years ago. Of the seven wonders of the ancient world, the pyramid complex is the only one that remains today.

The Great Sphinx of Giza sits near the pyramids and is one of the world's largest monuments. The limestone statue of a lion with a human head is 240 feet long and 66 feet tall.

The Great Sphinx

"HELLO" in Egyptian hieroglyphics

The ancient Egyptians developed a writing system more than 5,000 years ago.

It consists of pictures of people, animals, and objects, called hieroglyphs, that represent different words and sounds.

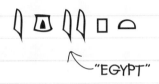

"EGYPT"

King Tut's tomb was discovered in 1922. The tomb's entrance had been hidden for 3,000 years. Items found inside included paintings, jewelry, statues, oils, and perfumes.

A gold coffin containing the mummy of King Tut was also found. Today visitors can see King Tut's gold death mask on display at the Egyptian Antiquities Museum in Cairo.

Blue Scarab Amulet Craft

Ingredients:

- [ ] ½ cup cornstarch
- [ ] ½ cup white glue
- [ ] 1 teaspoon white vinegar
- [ ] 1 teaspoon vegetable oil
- [ ] 3-5 drops blue gel food coloring
- [ ] 30-inch piece of yarn or string
- [ ] toothpick

Details:

Active Time: 30 minutes
Total Time: 24-48 hours

Make the Dough:

1. Stir the cornstarch and glue together in a microwave-safe bowl until smooth and creamy.

2. Add vinegar, oil, and food coloring to the bowl and mix the ingredients well.

3. Microwave on low for a minute, stirring halfway through. Be careful. The mixture will be hot.

Make the Amulet:

4. Let the clay cool for about five minutes. It should be warm (but not hot) to the touch.

5. Spread a few drops of vegetable oil on your hands and work surface. While it is still warm, knead the clay until it is smooth and free of lumps.

6. Roll out three balls: two the size of marbles and one the size of a pea. Flatten one marble-sized piece into an oval.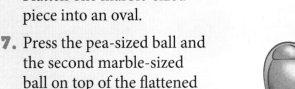

7. Press the pea-sized ball and the second marble-sized ball on top of the flattened oval to make a beetle shape.

8. Use the toothpick to draw a line across the beetle's abdomen. Draw a second line perpendicular to the first to make a T. Poke a small hole through the clay on each side of the beetle's head.

9. Allow the scarab beetle to air-dry for 24-48 hours until firm. Thread one end of the yarn or string through each hole and tie a knot. Enjoy your necklace!